☆ SPORTS STARS ☆

TIGER WOODS
DRIVING FORCE

BY MARK STEWART

ℚℙ Children's Press®
A Division of Grolier Publishing
New York London Hong Kong Sydney
Danbury, Connecticut

Photo Credits

Photographs ©: Allsport USA: 31, 35 bottom, 43 top (David Cannon), 3, 46 (J.D. Cuban), 43 bottom (Paul Devern), 27 (Rusty Jarrett), 9, 44 top left (Alan D. Levenson), 6, 14, 44 top right (Ken Levine), 10 (Gary Newkirk), 24, 47 (Jamie Squire); AP/Wide World Photos: 21, 40 (Curtis Compton), 17, 45 top left (Bob Galbraith), 23 (L.M. Otero), 13 (Amy Sancett), 41; Reuters/Archive Photos: 36 (Mike Blake), 32 (Allan Frederickson), 35 top, 39 (Gary Hershorn), 18, 45 top right (John Kuntz), 25 (Apichart Weerawong); SportsChrome East/West: 28 (Rob Tringali Jr.), cover (Michael Zito).

Visit Children's Press on the Internet at:
http://publishing.grolier.com

Library of Congress Cataloging-in-Publication Data

Stewart, Mark.
    Tiger Woods : Driving Force / by Mark Stewart.
        p. cm. — (Sports stars)
        Summary: A biography of Tiger Woods, son of an Asian mother and an African-American father and the youngest golfer ever to win the Masters Tournament.
        ISBN: 0-516-20971-X (lib.bdg.)   0-516-26424-9 (pbk.)
        1. Woods, Tiger—Juvenile literature. 2. Golfers—United States—Biography—Juvenile literature. [1. Woods, Tiger. 2. Golfers. 3. Racially mixed people—Biography.] I. Title. II. Series.
GV964.W66S84   1998
796.352'092—dc21
[B]—dc21   97-35340
                                                              CIP
                                                              AC

© 1998 by Children's Press®, A Division of Grolier Publishing Co., Inc.
All rights reserved. Published simultaneously in Canada.
Printed in the United States of America.
1 2 3 4 5 6 7 8 9 10 R 07 06 05 04 03 02 01 00 99 98

★ CONTENTS ★

Tiger and his parents, Earl and Kultida

NEW KID
ON THE BLOCK

Earl and Kultida Woods received a harsh welcome when they moved to the white, middle-class suburb of Cypress, California in 1975. They were the first people of color to move there and the first multiracial family that some of their neighbors had ever seen. Teenagers pelted their house with limes, rocks, and BBs and shattered their kitchen window.

Kultida, who was born and raised in the Asian country of Thailand, met Earl during the Vietnam War. Earl, an African-American, was a member of a U.S. army unit called the Green Berets. They fell in love, got married, and returned to the United States in 1969. Six years later, they had a baby boy and named him Eldrick—a made-up name that had an E for Earl at the beginning and a K for Kultida. That way, he would always have his parents at his side. Earl, however, preferred the name "Tiger." It was the nickname of a brave and heroic South Vietnamese officer name Nguyen Phong, who had been Earl's friend and had saved his life on more than one occasion.

Life for the Woods family got a little easier as time passed, but not much. Whenever they went shopping or took a walk, they felt the eyes of their neighbors upon them, and they could sense the hate. Tiger experienced this racial prejudice on his first day of kindergarten. Some older boys tied him to a tree, threw stones at him, and called him terrible names. This was not the first time Tiger had been singled out because of the color of his skin; it had also happened on the golf course.

Tiger was already an excellent golfer by this time. He took his first swing at the age of

Tiger has been an excellent putter since he was a kid.

10 months. At 18 months, Tiger was putting on the practice green and hitting tee shots at the driving range at the nearby Navy Golf Course (NGC). By the age of three, he was playing the course with his father. A local television station heard about Tiger and sent a news crew to film him. This led to an appearance on the *Mike Douglas Show*, where he put on a golfing exhibition with movie stars Bob Hope and Jimmy Stewart.

A remarkable young player, Tiger beat players twice his age.

Back at NGC, some members wanted Tiger off the course. They claimed that children should not be allowed to play, even though other kids were on the course all the time. Earl could not be sure, but he suspected that these were the same people who had made racist remarks to him when he first began playing NGC in 1975.

Tiger's father responded with an outrageous challenge. Tiger would play nine holes against the club's teaching pro. If the pro shot a better score, Earl and his son would leave the club. But if Tiger won, they would never be bothered again. The pro agreed. The match took place with Tiger hitting from the shorter ladies' tees and the pro hitting from the longer men's tees.

Tiger played perfectly; the pro did not, losing by
two strokes. Unfortunately, when club members
heard about the results, they claimed the pro
had no right to accept the challenge. They told
Earl that Tiger was still not allowed to play.

This turned out to be a blessing in disguise.
Tiger began playing the tiny Heartwell Park
course in Long Beach, where the distance
between the tees and the holes was much
shorter. This forced him to develop a "short
game" of approach shots, delicate chip shots,
and tricky shots out of sand traps. At Heartwell,
he also met his first coach, a man named Rudy
Durant. By the age of six, Tiger had been on
a prime-time national television show called
That's Incredible!, signed several autographs,
and had his first hole-in-one. He also won his
first international tournament.

★ 2 ★

TOURNAMENT TOUGH

When Tiger Woods turned seven, his father told him that he had the talent to do great things in golf. He also told Tiger that most talented golfers never achieved greatness. What they lacked, Earl explained, was mental toughness. For the next five years, Tiger's dad would do anything he could think of to distract him while he played. He would jingle his keys, drop his golf bag, roll a ball in front of him, or purposely break the rules when they played together. Earl promised Tiger that if he could survive this difficult training, he would never meet a tougher golfer. He also made sure not to push Tiger too hard—if he felt his son was about to cry, he would hold back.

Tiger's father has always taken an active role in making his son a great golfer.

"He tried to rattle me in every way he possibly could," says Tiger. "But he would never cross that point where I would break. Finally, one day it all of a sudden clicked, and he tried all his stuff and I just looked at him and smiled, and he knew it was all over." During this time Tiger entered more than two dozen tournaments a year. Although he usually was competing against older kids, he won with stunning frequency. In 1987, at the age of eleven, he won 30 events in a row!

At the age of 13, Tiger knew his future would be in golf.

★ ★ ★

By the time Tiger was 13, it was clear that his future was in golf. Besides a room full of trophies, he had a coach, a sports psychiatrist, and of course his dad, who had retired to work with him full-time after suffering a mild heart attack in 1986. Tiger also got his first college recruiting letter, from prestigious Stanford University in northern California.

Meanwhile, the mental training continued, but it now took a different path. Tiger's parents convinced him that he was going to be an important person one day. Tiger would be in a position to do some wonderful things both in and out of golf. That helped him deal with problems he encountered on the golf course, because he viewed each setback as something he could learn from, not something to be ashamed of. In Tiger's mind, his destiny was set—all that remained was the journey.

★ ★ ★

Tiger's first big win came at the 1991 United States Golf Association (USGA) Junior Championship, an event open to players 17 years old and under. Tiger, just 15, became the youngest champion in tournament history with a thrilling victory on the first hole of sudden death. In 1992, Tiger began working with Butch Harmon, a famous "swing doctor" who helps some of the top professionals with their games. Tiger won the USGA Junior title again, making him the event's first two-time winner. Later that summer, he was invited to play in the Los Angeles Open, making him the youngest player ever in an official Professional Golf Association (PGA) tournament. At the 1993 USGA Junior, Tiger roared back from a big deficit to pull even on the final hole and then won an unprecedented third title on the first hole of sudden death.

Tiger reacts after making a putt during the 1993 Los Angeles Open.

Tiger celebrates a winning shot with an uppercut swing.

⋆ 3 ⋆

AMATEUR HOUR

Tiger Woods accepted a scholarship from Stanford and prepared to take an important step in his career. For the next three years, he would juggle a hectic schedule, which included going to class and studying, playing college tournaments, playing national amateur tournaments, and having a little time to himself to hang out with his friends or play video games.

Tiger's first goal was to win the U.S. Amateur title. He had entered this event three times before and had outplayed golfers three times his age. But this time he wanted to win the tournament. Tiger played well and reached the finals at Sawgrass, where he faced University of Oklahoma star Trip Kuehne. Kuehne built a five-shot lead after 24 holes of their 36-hole final, but Tiger came back, pulling even with two holes to play. On the final hole (the famous "island green," one of the toughest in the world), Tiger went for broke with a shot that even the top pros rarely try. He nailed it, avoiding the water by a couple of feet. Tiger's mother, who was watching him on television, fell out of her bed when she saw the shot land. Next, Tiger rolled in a difficult 14-foot putt to win the tournament. He celebrated his victory with a big uppercut, which has since become his trademark.

Tiger won the U.S. Amateur championship in 1995 and again in 1996, making him the first player since the legendary Bobby Jones to win a national title six years in a row. He played the 1995 Masters, golf's most prestigious event, and had the best score of all the amateurs who competed. And Tiger also played the British Open a couple of times, gaining important experience in one of golf's toughest "majors."

Tiger enjoys his first visit to the Masters in 1995.

During three years at Stanford, Tiger ranked among the top college golfers. As a junior, he won the NCAA championship and was named College Golfer of the Year. He also spent a lot of time in the weight room, adding layers of muscle to his lanky, broad-shouldered frame.

Something else he added was a huge following of fans. At most college and amateur events, crowds rarely total more than a couple of thousand people. When Tiger played, there were thousands of people in his gallery alone. They were not typical golf fans. In fact some knew almost nothing about the game. They were turned on by Tiger and came to watch him play. When he made great shots, they cheered like fans at a football game. When he made poor shots, they shouted encouragement. Golf had never seen anything like this before.

After winning the 1996 U.S. Amateur, Tiger announced that he was leaving college and turning pro. College golf was becoming boring,

Tiger is surrounded by autograph seekers and fans wherever he plays.

and he had already defeated the best amateurs in the world. Considering how rapidly his body had developed, there seemed to be nothing stopping him from joining the professional tour. "It was time for me to go," he says, "and I was ready to go."

Tiger advertises for several major companies, such as Nike.

Luckily, money would not be a problem. Two of golf's biggest sponsors, Titleist and Nike, signed Tiger to multimillion-dollar deals to endorse their products. Each company predicted that Tiger was going to be golf's next superstar. And because of his multi-racial background, they hoped that he would attract people to the game of golf who had never considered playing it before. Most golf in the United States is played far from the inner cities, and most golf clubs are very expensive to join. For these reasons, among others, the vast majority of golfers today are white. Tiger hopes that his success will help change the face of golf.

Actually, Tiger would like people of all races to enjoy the game. Indeed, he constantly reminds his fans and the press that he himself is a representation of many races—not just

African-American, as he is often called. In terms
of Tiger's ethnic mix, few people realize that he
is actually more Asian than he is African. His
mother is one-half Thai, one-quarter European,
and one-quarter Chinese. His father is one-eighth
Chinese, one-eighth American Indian, and
three-quarters African-American. It sounds
complicated, but Tiger has found a way of
cramming all of his ancestors into one handy
word. "Growing up," he smiles, "I came up with
this name: I'm a Cablinasian."

**Tiger hopes to expose people all over the world to golf. Here,
he gives a clinic while playing in Thailand's Honda Classic.**

★ 4 ★

TIGER JOINS THE TOUR

It is very unusual for a 20-year-old to compete on the PGA Tour. But Tiger Woods is not a typical 20-year-old. He had been playing and winning pressure tournaments since he was a child—more than 100 in all. The bigger the stakes, the better he played. From a technical standpoint, he was already much better than most players on the tour.

When Tiger swings, the head of his club travels more than 200 miles per hour. And the

Tiger has learned to cope with the pressures and disappointments of professional golf.

Tiger's swing is virtually flawless.

angle at which the club face meets the ball is almost perfect. This enables Tiger to out-drive other golfers by 30 to 40 yards off the tee. This in turn makes his next shot to the green much shorter, resulting in fewer mistakes and easier putts.

Tiger made his first appearance as a pro at the 1996 Greater Milwaukee Open (GMO). Normally, this is an unimportant stop on the tour. Only a handful of big-name stars show up and the crowds are normally small. Thanks to Tiger's presence, however, the GMO became an international event. Attendance tripled, and hundreds of reporters and camera crews showed up to see how Tiger would do. Between rounds, fans camped outside his hotel room, hoping to get a glimpse of him through the window. On the final day, he rewarded his fans by knocking in a hole-in-one. Tiger finished 60th.

It might have been the first time that a player finishing 60th in an event made bigger news than the tournament winner.

Tiger made his major breakthrough less than two months later, at the Las Vegas Invitational. After shooting an average first round, he played the final three rounds in a stunning 26 shots under par. Beginning the last day, Tiger was seven strokes down to superstar Davis Love III. Tiger clawed his way into a tie on the last hole and then defeated Love on the first hole of sudden death. A couple of weeks later, Tiger won again at the Walt Disney World/Oldsmobile Classic in Orlando, Florida. He was presented with his winner's check by—who else?—Tigger!

One of the biggest adjustments golfers have to make after turning professional is learning how to relax. In Tiger's case, much of the stress and strain of making big decisions and living life on the road was being shouldered by his father.

Tiger plays a shot out of a sandtrap and onto the green.

Declining health has kept Earl Woods from walking the course with Tiger during tournaments.

★ ★ ★

It never occurred to Tiger that Earl might not be holding up—he seemed so calm and in control. But during the next tournament his dad suffered another heart attack and was rushed to the hospital. Earl required surgery but would recover, although doctors said it might be a very long time before he could walk 18 holes with Tiger again.

Despite this setback, Tiger's first year as a pro was a total success. He was even named 1996 PGA Tour Rookie of the Year. "I accomplished every goal I wanted and exceeded a couple," he says. "My main goal was to make the Top 125. I went beyond that."

★ 5 ★

MASTER BLASTER

Tiger Woods began the 1997 season with a new and ambitious plan. He wanted to win the Masters. The tournament's long holes and fast greens were suited to his game. When he arrived at the famed Augusta, Georgia, course, all anyone could talk about was whether Tiger could actually win. Most people thought it would be impossible. He was only 21 (most golfers do not play their best until they turn 30) and he had not played a major tournament since he turned pro. Could he win his first one?

At first, the answer appeared to be no. On the tournament's first nine holes, Tiger made four bad tee shots and ended up with a score of 40. No one had ever won the Masters after

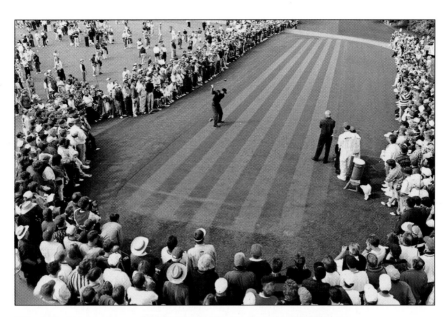

Tiger takes a practice shot before the 1997 Masters.

Tiger's great mechanics allowed him to bounce back from his shaky opening at the 1997 Masters.

Tiger tries not to look at the leader board, which shows a nine-shot lead over his nearest challenger.

such a poor start. But Tiger shortened his swing and made some clutch putts to achieve a score of 30 on the final nine holes. Just like that, he was back in the tournament. Tiger continued playing well and had the best score of the day for the second round. As the third round started, he held a three-stroke edge over his nearest challenger. He had proved he could take a lead at the Masters; now he needed to show he could hold it.

And hold it he did. In one of the most spectacular rounds of golf ever played, Tiger did not make a single mistake. He shot a 65 while everyone else was struggling to stay under 80. When the day was finished, he was nine shots ahead of the pack with just 18 holes to go. That evening, the clubhouse at Augusta was a very strange place. Usually, on the night before the final round, it is very tense and quiet. Everyone is thinking about the task that lies ahead. But with Tiger so far in front, the other golfers had no chance of winning, so they relaxed and enjoyed watching history being made.

★ ★ ★

Everyone agreed that Tiger was a breath of fresh air to a game that had begun to appear bland and stale. There is so much money in golf today that someone can actually become a millionaire without winning a single event. On a tournament's last day, many players are just trying to make sure they play safely— winning is not as important as finishing among the leaders and cashing a fat paycheck. Tiger, on the other hand, will do whatever it takes to give himself a chance to win. He tries risky shots, and he plays very aggressively. "Why go to a tournament if you're not going there to win?" he wonders. "Second stinks, and third's even worse!"

Back in his hotel room, Tiger's father told him the next day's round would be the toughest of his life. Everyone on the course would be watching him, expecting him to be perfect again, and rooting for him to break all sorts of records. It would be noisy and confusing. If he let any of this distract him, Earl warned, the results could

Tiger is a fearless and aggressive shot-maker.

be disastrous. Then they smiled at each other,
because they knew all that mental toughness
training was about to pay off.

Tiger played the front nine holes in the
required number of strokes. On the eighth hole,
he sank a long rolling shot that seemed to lock
him in for the rest of the day. From that point
on, Tiger was practically perfect. When he tapped
in his final putt on 18, he was the proud owner

LEADERS

PRIOR	HOLE	1	2	3	4	5	6	7	8	9	10	11	12	13	14	15	16	17	18
	PAR	4	5	4	3	4	3	4	5	4	4	4	3	5	4	5	3	4	4
15	WOODS	15	16	16	16	15	15	14	15	15	15	16	16	17	18				
6	ROCCA	6	7	7	7	7	6	6	6	6	6	5	5	5	5	5			
5	STANKOWSKI	5	4	3	2	2	2	3	3	2	3	2	2	2	3	3			
4	KITE T.	4	5	5	4	4	3	4	5	5	5	5	5	6	6	5			
4	WATSON. T.	5	6	6	6	7	6	3	4	4	5	5	6	6	6	6	5		
3	SLUMAN	3	3	3	3	2	2	3	3	3	3	3	3	4	5	3	3		
1	LOVE	0	1	0	0	1	0	0	0	0	0	0	1	3	3	4	3	3	
2	LANGER	2	1	2	2	2	2	1	0	1	0	0	0	1	1	2	2	2	2
2	COUPLES	2	3	3	3	2	1	2	2	2	2	2	2	3	1	1	2	3	
0	TOLLES	0	1	2	2	2	2	2	1	2	2	2	2	3	3	4	5	5	5

Tiger ignores the pressure on his way to establishing the best Masters score ever.

of the best Masters score ever. He ended up with an 18-under-par 270. Waiting for his son with a big bear hug was Earl Woods. It was one of the most emotional moments of his life. "It was the first tournament he was able to go to since his surgery," says Tiger. "It was nice to have him back on the team."

After the Masters, much was made of the fact that Tiger was the first African-American golfer to win the tournament. As always, he downplayed his historical significance and reminded reporters that he was a mix of many different races. But Tiger knew what the score was. In fact, he had dressed that morning in a red shirt

Tiger hugs his father after winning the Masters.

and black pants, fully aware that as the winner he would receive a ceremonial green jacket. Green, red, and black are the colors of African nationalism.

Since his victory at Augusta, Tiger has settled into life as the most-watched player on the PGA Tour. He has won a few more tournaments and finished off the pace in others. But every time he squeezes off one of his 330-yard drives, he strikes a blow for all of the things that make him special. "Golf is basically a vehicle for me to help people," Tiger explains. "I can inspire lives in a positive way. As long as I can touch one person, I feel I've done my job. But I'm definitely going to try to do a whole lot more than that."

Tiger Woods is young, confident, and sees himself as part of a bigger, more important picture. And even though he will always be described as African-American, in a very special way he is perhaps the most American golfer of all.

Wearing the green jacket and holding the trophy, Tiger savors his victory.

Tiger is confident that his future will be even brighter than his past.

C ★ H ★ R ★ O ★ N

1975 • December 30: Eldrick "Tiger" Woods is born in Cypress, California.

1991 • Tiger wins the United States Golf Association (USGA) Junior Championship for the first time.

1992 • Tiger is invited to play in the Los Angeles Open, making him the youngest player ever in an official Professional Golf Association (PGA) tournament.

1993 • Tiger wins the USGA Junior Championship for the third time in a row.

1994 • Tiger wins the U.S. Amateur Championship.

1995 • Tiger plays in the 1995 Masters Tournament and finishes with the best amateur score.

O ☆ L ☆ O ☆ G ☆ Y

1996
- Tiger wins the U.S. Amateur Championship for the third time.
- Tiger leaves Stanford University to join the pro tour.
- At his first appearance as a pro at the Greater Milwaukee Open (GMO), Tiger draws record crowds.
- Tiger is named PGA Rookie of the Year.

1997
- Tiger wins the Masters Tournament and establishes a record score.
- Tiger finishes as the PGA Tour's top money winner, and becomes the first golfer to win $2 million in a season.

Date of Birth
December 30, 1975

Place of Birth
Cypress, California

Height
6' 2"

Weight
160 pounds

CAREER HIGHLIGHTS

Three-Time U.S. National Junior Champion

Three-Time U.S. National Amateur Champion

1996 NCAA Champion

1996 College Player of the Year

1996 PGA Tour Rookie of the Year

1997 Masters Champion

1997 AP Sportsman of the Year

1997 PGA Tour Player of the Year

★ ★ ★

ABOUT THE AUTHOR

Mark Stewart grew up in New York City in
the 1960s and 1970s—when the Mets, Jets, and
Knicks all had championship teams. As a child,
Mark read everything about sports he could lay
his hands on. Today, he is one of the busiest
sportswriters around. Since 1990, he has written
close to 500 sports stories for kids, including
profiles on more than 200 athletes, past and
present. A graduate of Duke University, Mark
served as senior editor of *Racquet,* a national
tennis magazine, and was managing editor
of *Super News*, a sporting goods industry
newspaper. He is the author of every Grolier
All-Pro Biography and eight titles in the
Children's Press Sports Stars series.